Roy.

Please renew or return items by the date
shown on your receipt

www.hertsdirect.org/libraries

Renewals and   0300 123 4049
enquiries:

Textphone for hearing   0300 123 4041
or speech impaired

D1363055

520 739 76 3

Published by Puffin 2014
A Penguin Company
Penguin Books Ltd, 80 Strand, London, WC2R 0RL, UK
Penguin Group (USA) Inc., 375 Hudson Street, New York 10014, USA
Penguin Books Australia Ltd, 707 Collins Street, Melbourne, Victoria 3008,
Australia (A division of Pearson Australia Group Pty Ltd)
Canada, India, New Zealand, South Africa

Written by Richard Dungworth
Illustrated by Richard Jones – Beehive Illustration Agency

www.puffinbooks.com

ISBN: 978-0-14135-433-0
001
Printed in Great Britain

MIX
Paper from
responsible sources
FSC™ C018179

THE BLACK KNIGHT

CHARLIE PEPPER

PUFFIN

Contents

Prologue

Tenoroc bounded up the stone steps that climbed to the top of Temple Mount. His cape billowed behind him. As he reached the summit, he turned to confront his pursuer. He held up the black cloth bag he was clutching in one gnarled hand, and dangled it teasingly at arm's length.

'Is *this* what you're looking for, Hatter?' he sneered.

As Tenoroc faced him, Alfred Hatter halted on the steps below. The silver-haired adventurer met his enemy's mocking gaze with a steely look.

'If you release those prisoners, Tenoroc,' he replied, 'the Multiverse will crumble!'

Tenoroc's evil grin grew wider. 'It *needs* to crumble, Hatter! So *I* can pick up the pieces, and rebuild it – in *my* image!'

His challenger's face darkened. 'I can't let you do that,' he growled.

Tenoroc gave a snort of contempt. 'Try and *stop* me!'

Alfred was determined to do just that. Without hesitation, he started up the final flight of steps. In response, Tenoroc reached under his cape, snatched a fiercely spiked throwing weapon from his side and launched it viciously in Alfred's direction.

The fearless old adventurer dived out of the missile's path. Its lethal spikes lodged in the stone beside him. Within moments, he was back on his feet – and back on the attack.

Tenoroc, however, simply stood his ground, chuckling nastily. With a flick of his outstretched hand, he retrieved his weapon. It jerked free from the stone and flew straight back into his grasp. He hurled it at his defenceless enemy again. This time, Alfred's heroic efforts to avoid it sent him sprawling on his back.

Once more, Tenoroc used his powers to retrieve the weapon. He leisurely prepared to launch a third – and final – attack. Revelling in his victory, he threw back his head and let out a burst of scornful laughter.

'MWAA-HA-HA-HA – *OOOFF*!'

Tenoroc's triumphant cackle was cut short by something hitting him hard in the stomach. His determined opponent had somehow recovered quickly enough to catch him off-guard with a fierce headlong charge. Its force carried them both over the Mount's parapet. Grappling wildly, they plunged together into the abyss beyond.

It was only as they fell that Tenoroc realized his enemy was not unarmed after all. Alfred had a small hollow sphere, made up of many hexagonal faces, clutched in one hand. It pulsed with golden light. Horror flooded through Tenoroc as he recognized it.

'*NOOOO*!'

He had long known that Hatter was determined

to defeat him – but he had never dreamt that to do so, his old foe was even prepared to sacrifice *himself* . . .

Before Tenoroc could stop him, Alfred had smashed the Prison Orb against his caped back. There was a burst of light. In an instant, the Orb expanded, transforming into a spherical cage that enclosed them both. Within another split second, it divided into two. The enemies were torn apart, to become separately imprisoned in identical twin spheres.

Tenoroc clawed at the golden bars of his own cage, his face twisted with fury. He let out a roar of helpless rage as his vision blurred, his other senses became hazy, and he felt himself no longer falling but rising . . . higher . . . higher . . .

With a sickening jolt, Tenoroc came to. He was slumped forward over a shelf of cold rock. His grey-green skin was drenched in sweat. He lifted his head slowly, looked around, and groaned.

Even though much time had passed since the fight on Temple Mount, the pain of his defeat felt fresh and raw – as it did every time he relived the battle in his feverish dreams.

The weapon he had used that fateful day lay within his reach now. It stood on one spiked end on the flat rock before him. Its body was made up of three transparent orbs, and tipped with ferocious prongs. This was Tenoroc's Triple Sphere. As well as being his weapon of choice, it was the device through which he channelled his mystical powers.

Tenoroc reached out a long bony finger to touch the largest of the Sphere's orbs. A 3D image instantly appeared within it. It showed a statue – a stone likeness of his old foe. Tenoroc glared at it with hatred in his yellow eyes.

'Curse you, Alfred Hatter!' he hissed.

He drew himself up to his full terrible height,

clenched his fists, threw back his head, and gave a bloodcurdling yell.

'*Curse you for stranding me in this lifeless prison dimension!*'

The mist around him swallowed his angry cries. The Sky Prison in which Tenoroc was trapped did indeed seem a lifeless place. It was little more than an island of bare rock, surrounded by an endless sea of poisonous cloud.

But Tenoroc was not, in fact, alone.

'*Lifeless*, master?' squawked a high-pitched voice.

A strange beast crouched nearby. It was a small, ugly creature, with a flat nose, spiky head-crest, stubby tail and tiny wings. The colour and texture of its peculiar body were remarkably like those of the rocks surrounding it. It was a living gargoyle.

The creature scuttled towards Tenoroc with a look of puppyish eagerness. 'You're forgetting *me*!' it croaked.

Tenoroc scowled at the grovelling gargoyle.

'Craw,' he snarled, 'it's the thought of sharing eternity with *you* that holds a very *special* torment!'

The gargoyle considered this for a moment or two – then decided he had just been paid a compliment. 'Aw, gee!' he said, looking pleasantly embarrassed. '*Thanks*!'

Tenoroc shook his head despairingly. It was hard to believe that he, the all-powerful Tenoroc, terror of the Multiverse, had come to *this* – trapped beyond hope of escape, with only a pathetic, dim-witted underling like Craw for company. He knew he had only one man to thank for his downfall. Alfred Hatter. He turned his livid eyes back to the image in the Triple Sphere.

'Still,' growled Tenoroc, 'knowing that Hatter is trapped as well is *some* consolation.'

His gaze moved to what lay next to the Triple Sphere. Scattered across the table of rock was a collection of thin, gold-edged, hexagonal discs. A black cloth bag lay beside them.

'And *I* . . .' Tenoroc's thin lips curled in a sneer. '*I* have the Life Cells I stole from the *Chronicles*, each one of which contains a fearsome Super Villain!'

Tenoroc raised his monstrous hands, palms

upward. In response, the Life Cells rose too. As they floated into the air, they fanned out in front of Tenoroc. He began to browse them hungrily. Within each cell, a ghoulish figure stared back at him.

'Who shall be the first to do my bidding?'

He considered the fanged, black-caped occupant of one Life Cell.

'Vampire . . .?'

He turned his attention to the next Cell. It showed the scowling face of a woman – a woman with writhing serpents in place of hair.

'Medusa . . .?' pondered Tenoroc.

As his eyes fell on a third Cell, his cruel smile widened.

'Ah! *Yes*!' he hissed. 'The *ultimate* warrior!'

Tenoroc swept a hand through the air. The chosen Life Cell floated smoothly across to hover directly above the Triple Sphere. It settled into a hexagonal socket in the device's flat upper surface. As it locked into place, power from within the Sphere began to stream through it.

Craw was watching eagerly. He strained to see whose Life Cell his master had selected. As the Sphere's beam flooded through the Cell, the figure from within it slowly became visible as a faint, shimmering hologram suspended above it.

Craw's face filled with awe. He gave a dry gulp.

'*I summon . . .*' chanted Tenoroc, yellow eyes burning. He swept his fingers downwards. The holographic figure plunged through its Life Cell, through the Triple Sphere's upper globe, into the heart of the main orb. A flare of crackling green light exploded within the crystal.

'. . . *THE BLACK KNIGHT*!'

The peace and quiet of dusk had fallen over Harmonia Piazza. Only one figure was still about at this late hour – Alfred Hatter, sculpted in stone, stood proudly at the Piazza's centre.

A shadow began to creep over the statue. A thick bank of grey cloud was rapidly forming in the darkening sky. It smothered the light of the twin moons. The cloud rolled and shifted, slowly transforming into a horrifying likeness of a demonic, masked face.

Not far from the Piazza, a patch of air began to ripple and stretch, as though something was trying to break through. A moment later, a nightmarish figure materialized in mid-air – a giant of a man, wearing a helmet and suit of black armour, and riding a flying robotic horse.

The fearsome warrior reined in his Hover-Charger. He raised his visored face to the sky. In a voice as formidable as his appearance, he let out a grim cry of triumph.

'Lord Tenoroc – you are victorious!'

Tenoroc's cloud-image scowled down from above. His cruel voice came thundering through the chill night air.

'With Alfred Hatter gone, the Multiverse is mine for the taking!' it rumbled. 'Ride, Black Knight! Ride, and spread darkness throughout the lands – *IN MY GLORIOUS NAME*!'

The Black Knight responded with a mighty roar. He turned his Hover-Charger to face the Piazza, raised the hilt of his Laser Lance and activated its deadly beam. With another bellow, he urged his robotic horse forward. As he bore down on the Hatter Statue, he levelled his glowing lance. One fearsome blow sent the stone likeness of the Multiverse's saviour crashing to the ground.

1
The Famous Coronet

Matt gave the taxi driver a wave as the black cab pulled away. He turned to gaze up at the grand building behind him, and felt a thrill of excitement. It had been a long, tiring journey – but they were here, at last.

His dad was beaming. 'Here we are, Hatter family,' he said proudly. 'London's famous Coronet Movie Theatre – our new home!'

'Cool!' said Matt. His mum said nothing.

Matt still couldn't quite believe they were actually going to live here. It had been tough saying goodbye to his friends back in New York. He knew it would take time to get used to a different school, a different neighbourhood – a whole different *country*. But how many thirteen-year-old boys got the chance to live in a movie theatre? And not just any old theatre, either.

'The *Notting Hill Coronet*?' Zach had said, wide-eyed, when Matt told him the news. 'You're kidding, right? I mean, *zillions* of the best monster movies had their premieres at the Coronet!' Matt's best friend was almost as big a movie fan as Matt was. 'The place is *legend*!'

Matt didn't need telling. He knew all about the old London theatre, both from his dad's memories of growing up there, and from the stories his grandfather had told him, whenever he came to visit, of its glorious past. He knew that the Coronet had been run by Hatters for generations; that his own great-grandfather, Samuel Hatter, had installed its first movie projector, a century ago; and that in its glory days, the theatre had screened hundreds of classic movies. They included every one of Matt's personal top fifty, from *Night of the Minotaur* to *The Revenge of Redbeard*.

If leaving his New York life behind meant having the chance to help his grandfather run the Coronet, it was worth it.

Matt couldn't wait to see Grandpa again. He grabbed his own suitcase with one hand and, with the other, reached down for the much smaller case beside it. This tiny piece of luggage belonged to the one friend Matt had *not* had to leave behind. Marlon, his dwarf Tasmanian devil, had made the journey to London with him. The little furry ball of mischief was Matt's faithful companion (or 'partner in crime', if you asked Matt's mum). He scampered

along beside Matt now, chittering excitedly as they hurried up the steps to the Coronet's main entrance.

Matt's dad was already tugging at the handles of the theatre's double doors. He looked puzzled.

'What's the matter, Harry?' asked his wife.

'It's locked. But it shouldn't be. Dad always opens up first thing.'

There was no doorbell, so Matt's mum rapped on the glass pane. They waited a little while, then she knocked again. There was still no answer.

Matt's dad stroked his chin, looking thoughtful. 'I suppose I *could* try making a lock-pick out of something . . .' he muttered.

'Your father doesn't keep a spare key anywhere, then?'

'Of course! Good thinking, Meg!' Matt's dad looked at his wife as if she was a genius. 'Now, if I remember rightly, we used to hide it under *here* . . .' He bent down to lift one corner of the doormat – and retrieved an old brass key from beneath it.

Nice work, Mom, thought Matt. His scatterbrained dad was the inventive dreamer of the family, but when common sense was called for, it was his mum – a capable, practical, down-to-earth New Yorker – who came into her own.

Beaming once more, Matt's dad unlocked the

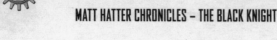

double doors, pulled them open with a flourish, then eagerly followed Matt and Marlon as they ducked through. His mum brought up the rear. Once inside the theatre's lobby, Matt dumped the cases and gave a cheery call.

'Grandpa!'

There was no response, so he tried again.

'Grandpa?'

His grandfather still didn't show. *Not to worry,* thought Matt – *he's probably busy somewhere.* He hurried after Marlon, who had scampered off in the direction of a popcorn machine perched on the lobby's ticket counter.

Matt's dad frowned. 'I don't understand,' he muttered. 'I'm *sure* Dad said he'd be here to meet us.'

Matt's mum was busy taking in their surroundings – with increasing dismay. The lobby looked as if it hadn't seen signs of life in a while. There was a pile of unopened post below the letterbox. A large pot plant in one corner was dry and shrivelled from lack of water. The ticket counter was thick with dust.

Meg looked at her husband, and raised her eyebrows.

'We came all the way from New York to Notting Hill – for *this*?'

From the theatre's abandoned air, she was willing to bet her father-in-law had gone off on another of his spur-of-the-moment, far-flung adventures.

Matt came racing back over.

'Yeah! Isn't it *amazing*?'

His mum could see from the sparkle in his eyes that Matt's first impression of the Coronet was very different from her own.

'C'mon, Marlon!' Matt sprinted over to the double doors on the far side of the lobby. 'Let's explore!' He burst through the doors into the corridor beyond, his little fur-ball of a friend hot on his heels.

2
Where's Grandpa?

The Coronet was everything Matt had dreamt it would be, and more. As he and Marlon explored the old theatre's corridors and cubbyholes, his liking for his new home grew stronger by the second.

Most of the ground floor was taken up by the lower level of the big Screen One auditorium. Here, tiers of stall seats curved around the vast, velvet-draped cinema screen itself. Matt sank into one of the red plush chairs. He imagined the theatre full, every member of the audience's gaze fixed on the dazzling screen, the smell of fresh popcorn in the air . . .

'How neat is *this*, Marlon?' he beamed.

The little Tasmanian devil was jumping up and down on the neighbouring seat, trying to flap it down. Matt gave him a hand. He twisted round to look up at the overhanging balcony, where there were more banks of scarlet seating. *You'd get an awesome view from up there, front row,* thought Matt. That's where he'd sit to watch his first movie . . .

Further back, and even higher up, he spotted a small square opening in the auditorium's rear wall.

'That's the window of the Projector Room,' he told Marlon. 'C'mon – let's get up there! Grandpa's probably fixing the projector or something!'

They hurried off in search of the stairs to the first floor. A wrong turn led them instead to the theatre's storeroom. For a movie fan like Matt, it was like finding Aladdin's cave.

'Just look at all this stuff!'

Metal film canisters stood in stacks, waist-high. Matt recognized most of the titles on their labels. There was a whole hoard of exciting movie memorabilia – a massive club hammer that looked just like the one wielded by the monster in

Eye of the Cyclops; a flame-red wig that Matt was sure belonged to his all-time favourite bad guy Flint Phoenix; a cool tailored jacket identical to the one Count Venom wore. There were even some ancient stage props from the Coronet's pre-cinema days.

'Hey, check *this*, Marlon . . .'

Matt lifted a moth-eaten screen drape to reveal another wonder – an old, twin-reeled movie projector, with one of its four legs missing. Marlon chittered appreciatively.

If Matt hadn't been so keen to find his grandfather, he would have happily spent hours rooting through the storeroom's treasures.

They found the stairs at their next attempt. But Matt's grandfather wasn't in the Projector Room – or anywhere else on the first floor. So they climbed a cool spiral staircase to the next level. This storey of the building was where Matt and his parents were to set up home. There was a kitchen, a living area and a little bathroom. Matt loved it all.

But the area he liked best by far, the place that really blew him away, was the room he and Marlon discovered last. The spiral staircase's final flight led up into a circular room with windows all around and a high domed ceiling. This was the interior of the Coronet's third floor turret.

'Whoa! This is *way* cool!' Matt scrambled up the steps to the raised sleeping platform and threw himself on to the big double bed. Marlon flopped

down next to him. They lay on their backs, gazing in awe at the arched ceiling. 'This is *so* gonna be *our* room!'

Their whirlwind tour of the Coronet had confirmed Matt's hopes – it was the best home a movie-mad teen could wish for. But despite all the theatre's delights, there was one vital thing missing. Matt made his way slowly back down the spiralling steps. As he descended to the first floor landing, he shook his head, and let out a sigh of frustration.

'I don't get it, Marlon . . .'

The little rodent went whizzing past Matt, riding the curved bannister like a helter-skelter. He squealed with delight as he shot off the end and flew across the landing.

'We've looked *everywhere*,' Matt went on, 'but there's no sign of –'

He broke off. He stood at the foot of the staircase, staring.

'*Grandpa?*'

3
The Hidden Door

Several pictures hung on the Coronet's first floor landing wall. It was one of these that had caught Matt's eye. It was a painted portrait of a white-haired gentleman. He had an impressively bushy moustache, and eyebrows to match. He was wearing a waistcoat, kilt and round-framed glasses, and had an explorer's hat tucked under one arm. It was an excellent likeness of the real Alfred Hatter, Matt's grandfather.

Matt continued to stare at the portrait. He was sure he had seen its eyes glint.

'Huh?'

Matt followed his grandfather's fixed gaze – to

a bookcase built in to a nearby recess in the wall. He crossed the landing to take a closer look. The shelves held all sorts of reading material. Gold lettering on one book's spine declared it to be *A Complete History of Music Hall*. Wedged in alongside this was *The Projectionist's Handbook*. Here was *Exploring the Himalayas*, and here *Advanced Taekwondo*. And here, propped between two brightly coloured neighbours, was a battered brown volume with a broad leather spine . . .

'Is that . . .?' murmured Matt. He reached up to remove it from the shelf. His face lit up with delight. 'It *is*!'

There was no mistaking his grandfather's old book. It had a very distinctive design. Its brown leather binding was engraved with intricate patterns and edged with brass trim. It was held shut by a heavy clasp. And mounted on its front cover was a hexagonal amber gemstone, surrounded by six translucent segments, like glass.

Marlon was eager to know what Matt had found. He hopped up on to one of the bookcase's shelves and gave an enquiring trill.

'Grandpa used to read me amazing stories from this book when I was a kid!' Matt explained. He stared at the amber jewel in the cover. He remembered how, as a young child, he had often

thought he could see a faint yellow glow flickering within it.

He glimpsed the same strange glimmer now. It must be the way the gemstone caught the light. He reached for the cover-clasp, keen to take a look inside the book.

But before Matt could release the clasp, he was distracted by a sudden beeping noise. He looked up to see a flashing yellow light, blinking in time with the beeps. Both light and noise were coming from another amber jewel, set in the bookcase's wooden frame.

'Huh?' frowned Matt. 'What's that, Marlon?'

And then the entire bookcase was moving. It swivelled on the spot, spinning about like a revolving door. Its sudden rotation sent Marlon flying across the landing, squealing – and swept Matt, helpless, straight through the hidden opening behind it.

4
A Call for Help

The surprise shove in the back from the revolving bookcase sent Matt stumbling forward through the hidden doorway. His grandfather's old book was jolted from his grasp and tumbled to the floor.

Matt was now standing in a long, red-carpeted passageway. There were movie posters all along its walls. It was much like the other theatre corridors he and Marlon had already explored – except one end was sealed, right behind him, by the solid wooden back of the bookcase.

A corridor behind a revolving bookcase? thought Matt. *What's that all about?* At the other end of the passageway he could see double doors with round porthole windows. They looked just like the doors to the Screen One auditorium. *But there isn't* another *screen, is there?* His grandfather had certainly never mentioned it. And even if there *was* a Screen Two, why would its entrance be concealed?

The dropped book lay on the floor at Matt's feet, face up. The glow in its amber cover jewel was now undeniable. *That's* not *just a trick of the light*, thought Matt. He watched, transfixed, as the glow grew rapidly brighter. A beam of shimmering golden light suddenly shot out from the shining jewel. It was projecting something!

A flickering 3D image of a tiny figure appeared just above the book's cover. As the projection grew stronger and clearer, it rose to hover at Matt's eye-level – and he realized who he was looking at.

'*Grandpa?*'

The miniature hologram of his grandfather began to speak in a familiar Scottish accent. The sound was weak and a little fuzzy, but Matt could clearly hear the urgency in the old man's voice.

'I've barely enough power to send this message, so listen carefully! The fate of many worlds rests on *your* shoulders, Harry!'

Harry? Matt's head spun. That was his dad's name, not his!

'Grandpa – it's *Matt*!' he told the holographic figure. 'Where *are* you?'

Holo-Grandpa gave no sign of having heard him, and pressed on earnestly.

'We Hatters have a sworn responsibility to protect the Multiverse, and *you*, Harry, are the next Hatter Hero!'

'Hatter *hero*?' echoed Matt, baffled. 'What are you talking about?'

Once more, his grandfather ploughed on without answering.

'Harry, you *must* come to the Multiverse!'

There was that word again. *Multiverse*. Matt wondered what in the world that could be.

'A Tracker and Keeper will be there to guide and assist you. Have faith in them – *and* have faith in yourself!'

The projection's sound was starting to break up a little. The image began to slip in and out of focus.

'The Multivision Specs are in the *Chronicles*.'

The whosis *are in the* whatsis? thought Matt.

'Put them on and let them guide you here!' urged his grandfather's dwindling voice. 'Hurry! Time is running out . . .'

Matt watched helplessly as the projection faded fast.

'No – don't go! Grandpa!'

The light from the amber jewel died, and the hologram vanished.

Matt snatched up the book from the floor. He held it in front of him, yelling at its cover.

'*Grandpa*? *GRANDPA*?'

None of what Matt had just heard made any sense, but he was sure of one thing. His grandfather was in some sort of trouble.

'Can you hear me?'

Matt stared into the amber jewel, as though hoping to see his grandfather within. Instead, he saw the gemstone begin to glow more brightly again. The six clear segments around it were glimmering, too. Beneath their glassy surface, a complex clockwork mechanism had become faintly visible. Its ghostly cogs, springs and levers whirred and twitched into life.

'Whoa!'

Matt gave a startled yelp as the book's clasp suddenly clicked undone – and its cover swung open, unaided, in his palm.

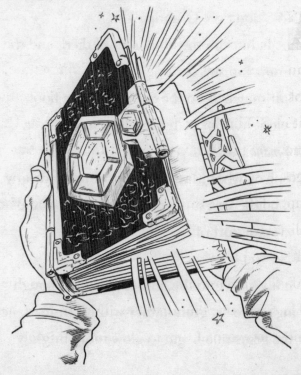

5
Through the Portal

As the pages of the old book spread themselves wide, golden light flooded out from within them. To Matt's astonishment, the book lifted gently from his hands. It tipped upright as it rose. Through screwed up eyes, Matt half-saw something swoop up, bat-like, from the blazing pages. It settled lightly on the bridge of his nose, wrapped its wings around his temples – and Matt realized what it was.

It was a pair of ultra-cool sunglasses. Instead of darkened lenses, these snazzy shades had one red lens and one blue, like the 3D specs Matt had sometimes worn at the movies. But no ordinary cinema specs had ever produced the effect that *this* pair did . . .

As they tucked snugly behind his ears, Matt felt a satisfying thrill run through his nervous system. It was as if a missing part of him had just been reconnected. The specs didn't just fit well – they felt like they *belonged* on him.

With them on, Matt found his vision transformed. He could look directly into the fiery pages of the floating book, which had now risen to hover right in front of his face. Its golden light no longer dazzled him.

Then, without warning, the book shot away from him. It rocketed along the corridor, leaving a trail of blue light in its wake. As it hurtled towards the double doors at the end of the passageway, they burst open to let it through. Before they swung closed, Matt caught a glimpse of an auditorium beyond, flooded with light. So there *was* a Screen Two!

Matt stared at the book's glowing trail. It hung in the air like luminous blue mist. Floating within it, spaced out along the corridor, were several faint holographic forms. The nearest one looked like a costume of some kind. Next came a pair of gloves. Hovering at the corridor's far end was a ghostly backpack. They had all emerged from the open book as it sped along the passageway.

'Whoa!'

Matt let out a startled cry as an invisible force seized hold of him. Unable to resist its pull, he found himself moving along the corridor. He started to jog, then broke into a run.

As he approached the first floating hologram, the strange force took full charge of Matt's body. He sprang into the air, diving acrobatically through the holographic costume. His head and arms slipped smoothly into its neck and sleeves.

In an instant, Matt's entire appearance was transformed, from schoolboy to hero. His everyday clothes were upgraded to cool new action gear – a top with an 'MH' logo, combat shorts and a pair of funky trainers.

Matt landed in skater stance, going into a long side-on slide. The strange force still had control of

his body. His hands swiped up at the holographic gloves – and he found himself wearing real ones.

A final leap and twist completed Matt's transformation. His arms slipped through the straps of the holographic backpack, and it too took solid form. He landed at a flat-out sprint and burst through the doors at the corridor's end.

Matt barely noticed what the interior of the

secret Screen Two auditorium looked like. He only
had eyes for the screen itself. It was ablaze with
purple light. It had become something other than
an ordinary cinema screen – a whirling, crackling
portal of luminous energy. Matt had no idea how it
had happened, or why. But he knew that it was this
that was pulling him in. His grandfather's book was
hovering at its very centre, its pages still open.

Matt raced down the sloping aisle to the front of the auditorium. He crouched down to spring, then launched himself into the air. As he dived headlong at the blazing screen, he made a grab for his grandfather's book – then disappeared into the whirlpool of purple light.

6

The Master Scholar

'Settle down, my friends! Settle down!'
The purple-robed Council elder, with
wild horns of white hair and a beard almost to his
waist, attempted to raise his voice above the din.
The crowd gathered around him in the cavernous
space of Harmonia's Central Hall were all talking
at once. The ancient scholar gazed at them through
his enormous spectacles. Despite his frailty, his eyes
shone with intelligence and energy. He clapped his
hands impatiently, and tried once again to restore
order.

'Please, my friends, a little quiet!' he squeaked.
'This is a time for calm and clear thinking!'

The hubbub slowly subsided. As a hush fell, a lone voice spoke out.

'Calm, Baccus? How can we be calm?' asked a man near the front of the crowd. 'The attack on Alfred Hatter's statue was worrying enough. Now there are messengers arriving by the hour with news of other violence outside the city. Harmonia has not seen such acts of destruction since . . . well, since . . .'

'Since Tenoroc was on the loose?' Baccus's blunt words sent another wave of nervous muttering rippling through the crowd. Baccus raised his hands, appealing once more for quiet. 'Yes, yes, Demetrius – I know what everyone is saying. That our old enemy is back.' He shook his head, then addressed the crowd earnestly. 'But I tell you now, my friends, that it cannot be so!'

Baccus's big round spectacles slipped a little. He pushed them back on to the bridge of his nose, and continued.

'As Harmonia's Master Scholar, I have made it my business to study Tenoroc's evil career in great detail. When our dear friend and protector Alfred Hatter fought his last epic battle with Tenoroc, on Temple Mount, he succeeded, as you know, in expelling him from our realm. Tenoroc was locked away in an isolated prison dimension. I do not believe that even Tenoroc – powerful as he is – could have escaped from his Sky Prison. I refuse to accept that he has returned to the Region of Ruins. Or, for that matter, that he has managed to break free into *any* of the Twelve Realms.'

Demetrius spoke up again.

'Then if not Tenoroc, who *is* responsible for these recent crimes?'

Baccus looked thoughtful for a moment or two.

'Tenoroc himself cannot be at large in our land, I feel certain. But that is not to say that he has no hand in these dreadful affairs. It is possible that even from exile he has found a way to exert his evil influence. I fear some agent of his – someone or something under his control – may be to blame for our current troubles. I fear that he may still possess the Life Cells . . .'

'And how will we meet this new threat, Master Scholar?' asked a woman beside Demetrius. 'We Harmonians are a peaceful people.'

'True, Philonella, true,' replied the old scholar. 'But this is not the first time we have faced peril. When Super Villains terrorized our realm in the past, were they not vanquished by a Hatter Hero? Samuel Hatter, and after him his dear son Alfred, never failed to come to our aid.'

'But Alfred Hatter sacrificed his own freedom to capture Tenoroc,' piped up another voice. 'He cannot help us now!'

'*Alfred* Hatter?' said Baccus. He shook his head sadly. 'No, he cannot . . .' Then his ancient face crinkled in a knowing smile. 'But perhaps the time is near when a *new* hero will take on the role of our protector. We must have faith, Samorus!'

At the fringes of the crowd, beyond the huddle of adults, stood two younger listeners. The taller of the two was a bright-eyed, crimson-haired girl. She wore a sleeveless purple martial arts-style outfit, which carried the Tree of Life emblem – the sign

of a Tracker. She had an ornate scabbard slung across her back, holding a short wooden staff. Atop the staff was an egg-shaped stone of smooth, polished amber.

'D'you hear that Gomez?' the girl whispered to the boy beside her. He was a little younger than her, dark-haired and dark-skinned. He was dressed in the green hooded tunic worn by all Keepers. 'Baccus thinks we're due a new Hatter Hero! If he's right, maybe you and I will get to see a little action at last!'

'You think, Roxie?' The boy's anxious expression suggested that he was in two minds about this prospect. 'What . . . like, *soon*?'

'Let's hope so!' said the girl. 'In the meantime, I for one don't intend to sit around twiddling my thumbs. We should at least try to get an idea of who we're up against. C'mon . . .' She turned her back on the crowd. 'Let's go take a closer look at that statue. Maybe we can find some answers . . .'

7
Tracker and Keeper

Roxie slipped out through the tall white columns of the Portico, the grand entrance to Harmonia's Central Hall. She was glad to get back out into the daylight and fresh air. A flight of stone steps led down from the Portico on to the Piazza – a wide, open paved area. Roxie took them two at a time, with Gomez right behind her.

Except for the Guardians – the two colossal stone figures who stood watch on either side of the Portico – the Piazza was deserted. Usually it was a popular public meeting place. But news of the attack on the Hatter Statue was keeping people away. The anxious Harmonians were staying in their homes. What if the shadowy figure who had been glimpsed fleeing the scene of the crime was to return?

The fact that a place so typically bustling with life had become so silent and empty made a chill run through Roxie's veins. She looked away into the distance, across the wide rocky chasm that lay beyond the Piazza, to the shadowy landscape on its far side. There, beyond the Broken Bridge, lay the dark, deserted land of Discordia. The Harmonian scholars said that it had once been as vibrant, as full of life and laughter, as their own land. Roxie shivered, and tried to turn her mind back to the task in hand.

The toppled statue lay next to its plinth in the centre of the Piazza. It was a double-size likeness of the great Alfred Hatter. Roxie hurried over to take a closer look.

Gomez sat down on the edge of the empty plinth to watch Roxie do her stuff. He could see from the concentration on her face that she was already in full-on Tracking mode. She was 'tasting'

the air around the statue, in a way that only a
Tracker could.

'Hmmm . . .'

Roxie looked thoughtful for a moment or two.
She lifted her chin and took in another long, slow
breath through her nose.

'Faint traces of *ozone* . . .'

Gomez seized his chance to show what *he* could
do. Everyone knew that Trackers were the best at
finding signs. But for interpreting those signs, you
couldn't beat having an encyclopaedic knowledge

of anything and everything concerning the Twelve Realms. That was when Keepers came into their own.

Gomez rifled through his vast mental store of facts, trivia and tidbits. What in the Multiverse could have left an ozone footprint?

Within moments, he had his answer.

'Electrostatic disrupter weapon,' he declared. 'Probably,' he added modestly.

Roxie crouched down beside the Hatter Statue and began to run her fingers and eyes over its stone surface, in search of more clues. She suddenly turned her attention to the Piazza pavement. She had spotted something – a drop of dark liquid. She dipped a fingertip into it and examined the slimy gloop more closely.

'Some kind of oil-based fluid . . .'

Once again, Gomez took only a moment or two to make a connection.

'A mechanical chariot,' he said, looking pleased with himself. 'Or maybe a Charger.' Then his smile vanished. His eyes grew wide with fear. It had just occurred to him what the two clues, taken together, might mean. In a trembling voice, he shared his upsetting deduction with Roxie.

'C-could be the B-B-Black Knight!'

Roxie came over to join Gomez. She didn't seem overly worried by his theory – just pleased to be making progress. 'I think we're getting the hang of this villain tracking!' she said cheerily. 'Maybe we sh–'

She broke off. A repetitive beeping had begun to sound just behind her left ear. Startled, she looked over her shoulder – to see the amber orb atop her staff blinking with yellow light.

Roxie quickly slid the staff from its sheath. She stared at the flashing jewel in disbelief.

'It *can't* be . . .!'

Gomez knew as well as Roxie what the jewel's behaviour meant. His heart swelled with excitement. Thoughts of the Black Knight were forgotten. He raised his eyes to the sky. Sure enough, one area of it was already beginning to shimmer and swirl. A portal was forming.

'The new Hatter Hero – at last!' cried Gomez. 'Roxie . . .'

Roxie, too, was gazing skyward, staring at the widening mouth of the portal. Her violet eyes sparkled.

'Gomez!' she whispered. 'This is where it all begins for us!'

Together, they watched the portal come snaking down out of the sky towards them, and waited for the arrival of the Multiverse's new champion.

8
Welcome to the Multiverse

The journey through the portal was a ride Matt wouldn't forget in a hurry. When he dived into the dazzle of the Coronet's Screen Two, he was swallowed by a tunnel of streaming purple light. His body hurtled along it, spinning uncontrollably. He quickly lost any real sense of up, down, left and right. One moment he was plummeting head first along the tube of rushing energy. The next, he was on his back, riding its twists and turns like a water slide – but unlike any slide Matt had been on before, this one thrashed about, like a living thing, as he zoomed along it. For a few exhilarating moments, he found himself on his feet, surfing the lightwaves, yelling with the thrill of it.

His stomach did yet another somersault. Up ahead, a circle of a more familiar kind of light was rapidly growing. Daylight.

A second later, the snaking tube of energy spat Matt out. He found himself flying through the air. This was *normal* falling now, forward and downward. The ground rushing up to meet him looked normal enough, too – hard, solid ground . . .

'Aaaaaaaaaaaaaaahhhhhhhhhhhhhhhh!'

Howling as he fell, Matt tried to summon all his skater skills to save his skin. *It's just a jump*, he told himself. *A big jump, maybe – but I can land it . . .*

He hit the ground, still travelling forward at quite a rate. His cool new trainers skidded across a smooth paved surface. Then they found their grip, and he went sprawling flat on his face.

'Whu-*ooooofff*!'

The crash landing, and the wild ride before it, left Matt dazed and confused. He was still getting used to the effect of the strange spectacles, too. He lifted his head weakly from the floor and tried

to shake it clear – then wished he hadn't. He was relieved to have stopped moving, at least.

Matt vaguely wondered who the two pairs of feet he was staring at belonged to. He looked up.

A crimson-haired girl, dressed in purple, and a boy in a green hooded tunic and head-band were peering down at him. The girl was frowning.

'No *way*!' she said, with evident disappointment. 'This *can't* be the new Hatter Hero. He's just a kid!'

Even in his fuddled state, Matt found this complaint a bit odd. The girl only looked about his own age. Her companion apparently agreed with him.

'In case you hadn't noticed,' Matt heard him whisper to the girl, 'so are *we*.'

The boy pointed a finger at Matt's face.

'Look – he has the Multivision Specs!'

On cue, the strange spectacles came to life. The nose-bridge split. The lenses slid smoothly apart with a *vzzzz-tk*! Matt felt a tiny click in each temple as the specs vanished. His vision returned to normal – only none of what he saw made sense. He *should* be inside the Coronet, but . . .

'What just happened?' mumbled Matt, struggling to get to his feet. The boy in the hooded tunic hurried to help him up. Matt gazed around, bewildered. 'What *is* this place?'

The boy gave a grand sweep of his arm. 'Welcome to the Multiverse!' he said, beaming.

Matt continued to gawp at his surroundings. This definitely *wasn't* Notting Hill.

He was standing at one end of a narrow stone bridge. A wide paved area spread out in front of him. At its far side loomed a high cliff-face, in which was set a grand pillared entrance. It looked rather like the front of one of the old temples Matt had seen in books on Ancient Greece. There were steps leading up to it, and a colossal statue on either side. Behind him, the bridge extended across a deep, sheer-walled canyon. A river of glowing red liquid – was that lava? – flowed slowly along the bottom of the chasm.

Lying only a few metres away, near the centre of the paved area, was something that made Matt stare and catch his breath.

'Hey! That's *Grandpa*!'

He rushed over to the fallen statue and knelt beside it. There was no doubt about it – it was a giant stone replica of his grandfather.

The two strangers had followed Matt over to the statue. The girl was frowning again.

'Alfred Hatter's your *grand*father?' she said, sounding puzzled.

Matt looked up at her, and nodded.

'Then it's skipped a generation!' cried the boy.

Matt didn't follow. But he could tell from the girl's expression that she wasn't too thrilled with this news.

'So, instead of Harry Hatter,' she said, 'The *Chronicles* sent us . . .?'

Matt got to his feet to introduce himself.

'Matt,' he said. 'Matt Hatter. I'm Harry's son.'

The boy and girl took a moment to process this.

'Look,' said Matt, 'rewind a minute . . .' He was still utterly confused. It felt like *he* should be asking the questions. There was a great deal he wanted to know: what he was doing here; where exactly 'here' was; and why in the world someone had built a giant statue of his grandfather. He decided to start with something simple.

'Who *are* you guys?'

The girl held her head high. 'The name's Roxana Alexis,' she told Matt proudly.

'Number one Tracker!'

'But you can call her Roxie,' added her younger companion. 'And I'm Gomez, last of the Keepers.' It was his turn to stand tall. 'I'm here to watch over you.' He gestured to Roxana Alexis. 'And her.'

Roxie gave him a withering look. 'You mean, you tag along for the ride!' she snapped.

'Ri-i-ght . . .' Matt sensed a slight difference of opinion. But he wasn't done asking questions yet. 'How come there's a statue of my grandpa?'

'Why wouldn't there be?' said Roxie. 'Alfred Hatter is the Multiverse's greatest hero!'

'O-kaay . . .' So far, Matt wasn't feeling any less confused. 'And what the heck is "the *Multiverse*"?'

Gomez gave another sweep of his arm.

'You're standing in it!' he replied. 'Or at least, one part of it. You see –'

Roxie cut him off.

'You've got the *Chronicles*, right?' she asked Matt. Seeing his blank expression, she tried again. '*The Interactive Chronicles of Action and Adventure*?' Matt continued to stare at her like she was talking gibberish.

From behind Roxie, Gomez was signalling for Matt to check his backpack. 'The big book!' he mouthed helpfully.

The penny dropped.

'*Grandpa's* book?'

Matt reached over his shoulder to slip the old book out of his recently acquired backpack – into which it fitted snugly. He looked at it with fresh interest. He couldn't remember his grandfather ever calling it 'the *Chronicles*'. But then he had never asked its title . . .

'Open it, Matt!' Gomez encouraged him. 'And you'll see the many wonders –'

He was cut short by Matt's whoop of astonishment.

'*Whoa!*'

Matt had followed Gomez's advice, and turned back the book's heavy cover.

9
A Reluctant Hero

As Matt opened *The Interactive Chronicles of Action and Adventure*, the Multivision Specs reactivated. They slid from nowhere – *vzzz-tk!* – to wrap around his eyes.

Looking down at the pages of the book, with the Specs on, was mind-bending. It was unlike any other reading experience Matt had ever had. 'Reading' wasn't even the right word. It was more like watching a movie – although that still didn't do it justice. It felt more active than just watching. Matt felt almost like he was part of the book.

The first image to fill the glowing pages was a bird's-eye view of the rocky landscape in which

Matt, Roxie and Gomez now stood. The lava-filled canyon, the pillared temple, the bridge on which Matt had crash-landed – all were spread out far below him.

'The Multiverse is a hidden dimension made up of many different realms . . .'

Gomez seemed somehow aware of what the book was showing Matt. As Matt stared in wonder, he listened to the young Keeper's commentary.

'The Region of Ruins . . .'

Matt felt like an eagle soaring high in the sky. From this vantage point, he could see that the bridge didn't reach the canyon's other side. It was broken. There was another temple, too – a small, round one, mounted on a tall pillar of rock in the centre of the canyon. Its domed roof sheltered a large sphere of pomegranate gemstone . . .

And then the book was taking Matt somewhere else completely. He was flying low over smooth golden dunes, zooming across a desert. A scorching sun blazed in the cloudless sky.

'The Sea of Sands . . .' he heard Gomez say.

The *Chronicles* carried Matt in a banking turn.
He went rushing past three giant, fierce-looking
reptiles dashing across the sand.

'*Wow*!' he murmured, spellbound. *Raptors*!
In the Multiverse, dinosaurs were evidently a lot
less extinct!

Now he was racing towards a walled desert
town, zooming through its open gates . . .

. . . and into sudden darkness. As his eyes
adjusted, he saw a city stretching out below him.
A network of bizarre aerial runways hung above
its shadowy streets, like a huge spider's web . . .

' . . . and Carnival City,' said Gomez.

The pages of the big book abruptly whited out.
A moment later, a tiny figure appeared at its centre.
It grew larger, striding out of the page towards
Matt. It was a man in a tailored gothic jacket.
He had red eyes, a jet-black bat tattoo on his pale,
bald head and *very* pointy teeth.

The vampire dissolved away. A second figure
approached. This time it was a hulking armoured
giant, with a single hideous mechanical eye . . .

'Wait!' cried Matt. 'I *recognize* these guys!'

The freakish parade continued – a woman with snakes for hair; a green-skinned youth tattooed with flames; a creature with the body of a man and the head of a bull – Matt had seen them all before . . . on the cinema screen! They were the bad guys from some of his favourite old movies. Medusa, Flint Phoenix, the Minotaur . . .

'You *should* recognize them, Matt!' confirmed Gomez. 'Long ago, these monsters and Super Villains leaked into the Multiverse from the place they call "the Coronet". They turned the Multiverse into a dark and dangerous place.'

Matt struggled to take in what Gomez was implying – that by screening films at the Coronet, his ancestors had somehow allowed their awesome movie villains to escape into another world. This world.

'So . . . villains from old scary movies . . . *came to life*?'

'That's right,' replied Gomez.

Matt shook his head. His great-grandfather Samuel Hatter had been known in his heyday as 'The Monster Maker', thanks to his tendency to screen mostly monster movies. Given what Matt had just learned, the nickname was highly appropriate.

'Your grandfather – and his father before him – journeyed to the Multiverse via a portal to try to recapture the escaped villains.'

Matt stared, transfixed, as the *Chronicles* began to display a silent, black-and-white flashback. He watched his grandfather take on a hideous monster wrapped head-to-toe in bandages – the Mummy from *Fate of the Pharaohs*! The gallant old adventurer seemed to be overpowering the monster with the fizzling beam of a hi-tech gadget grasped firmly in his outstretched hand.

'One by one,' continued Gomez, 'your grandfather locked them away in the *Chronicles*' Villain Vault.'

Before Matt could ask what Gomez meant by this, the content of the *Chronicles* changed abruptly again. Matt found himself staring at someone's caped back. Whoever it was seemed to sense the weight of Matt's gaze, and turned to confront him.

Matt's heart leapt into his throat. He had never seen anyone so terrifying before – even in a movie.

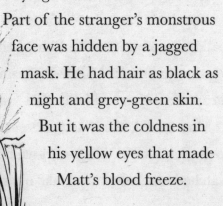

Part of the stranger's monstrous face was hidden by a jagged mask. He had hair as black as night and grey-green skin. But it was the coldness in his yellow eyes that made Matt's blood freeze.

Without warning, the demonic stranger lunged at Matt from within the *Chronicles*, clutching at him with long, gnarled fingers. Matt gasped, recoiled, and slammed the book shut. The Multivision Specs wiped off his face to reveal his blue eyes, wide with terror.

Gomez gave Matt a knowing look.

'I'm guessing you just met Tenoroc, Master of all Super Villains,' he said. 'And *your* arch-enemy!'

'*What?*' Matt looked aghast. 'I don't *want* an arch-enemy! Especially that guy!'

Roxie had been standing silently by for as long as she could bear. Now that she and Gomez had identified the villain responsible for wrecking the Hatter Statue, she was itching to go after him.

'You don't have a say in it, bone-brain!' she snapped at Matt. 'Look, there's been no trouble here in the Region of Ruins for quite some time – thanks to your grandfather. But now some maniac is on the loose. The Master Scholar thinks that Tenoroc might have set him free from a Life Cell. If that's true, only a Hatter can sort it out. Only *you –*' she prodded Matt in the chest – 'can capture Tenoroc's villains and return them to the Villain Vault!'

Deep down, Roxie understood that Matt needed time to adjust. But somehow she had expected the new Hatter Hero to be more . . . well . . . *heroic.*

'If it helps, Matt,' said Gomez sympathetically, 'you'll not meet Tenoroc face to face. He's locked away in a prison dimension. Your grandfather saw to that when they fought their final battle.'

Matt didn't like the sound of the word 'final'.

'What happened to Grandpa?' he asked anxiously.

Gomez frowned. 'I'm afraid he shared Tenoroc's fate, Matt. Your grandpa is trapped somewhere in the Multiverse, too – in another locked dimension.'

Then I'll find him and free him! thought Matt determinedly. He wouldn't let his grandfather down. But as for taking on Super Villains – that was a different matter. Roxie wasn't the only one struggling to see him as hero material. Matt felt well and truly out of his depth.

'*Dad* was meant to be this "Hatter Hero", not me!' he protested. 'I'll just give *him* the specs and –'

Gomez was shaking his head.

'You can't!' he told Matt. 'Once the Multivision Specs identify a Hatter's bloodline, they DNA-lock. They won't work on anyone but you now.'

Matt looked crestfallen.

Roxie's last drop of patience ran out.

'Quit dragging your feet and get with the programme!' she barked, giving Matt a fierce look. 'We've got a villain to bag!'

With that, she brushed past him, and strode purposefully away across the Piazza. Gomez and Matt exchanged glances, then followed in her wake.

'The last report of trouble came from one of the villages out on the plateau,' said Roxie as they fell in behind her. 'Near the gem mines. That'll be the best place to pick up a trail.'

The trio made their way along the cliff-side promenade, heading for the plateau. As they walked, Gomez couldn't resist getting to know the Multiverse's new celebrity a little better.

'Did I mention,' he whispered to Matt, 'that I'm also president of the Hatter Fan Club?'

'I have a fan club?' Matt raised an eyebrow. Then he grinned. 'Cool.'

Maybe having to be a hero wouldn't be *that* bad, after all . . .

10
The Black Knight's Mission

Tenoroc cursed as he felt his strength fail again. His control over the Triple Sphere faltered. The image within it became a blurry fuzz.

Releasing the Black Knight had taken far more out of Tenoroc than he had expected. He was shocked at how drained he felt. At the height of his powers, he could easily have freed every one of the Life Cells' Super Villains at once. But his imprisonment by Alfred Hatter had left him weaker than he had realized.

But not for long, thought Tenoroc. With the Life Cells in his control, he was confident that it was only a matter of time before he regained his full

powers and his freedom. *And then I will bring the people of the Multiverse to their knees . . .*

Rallied by these thoughts, Tenoroc channelled his will once more through the Triple Sphere. The image in its crystal orb came back into focus. It showed three young companions, heading out across the rocky landscape of the Region of Ruins. Tenoroc had watched their first meeting moments earlier with great interest. He recognized something familiar in the faces of both Tracker and Keeper. But it was the third youth – the bright-eyed, wild-haired boy with the backpack – who fascinated him.

Curse their wretched line! thought Tenoroc bitterly. He had hoped that Alfred Hatter would be the last of his kind. *The last interfering Hatter foolish enough to oppose me.* Now it seemed that his

old enemy had an heir, and that the Multiverse had chosen another champion from the Hatter bloodline. This infuriated Tenoroc. But as he studied the unremarkable boy in the Triple Sphere's orb, his fury quickly turned to contempt.

'So . . .' he hissed, sneering. 'The new Hatter is a mere *child*.'

Craw, Tenoroc's underling, was watching too. 'Insult!' he shrieked, hopping up and down with outrage. 'It's an *insult*, I say!'

Tenoroc ignored the gargoyle. 'Still . . .' he muttered to himself, 'a Hatter is a Hatter, and – boy or not – he must be destroyed!'

Tenoroc would have dearly liked to deal with his new enemy in person. But he knew that he must find another way. He had a faithful servant already at his disposal in the Region of Ruins. *Yes*, he thought spitefully, *a merciless warrior, famous for his supreme strength and skill, will be more than a match for a puny boy . . .*

The Black Knight reined in his Hover-Charger on the crest of the rocky slope. Through the eye-slits of his visor, he looked down at the cluster of dwellings below. It was a small mining village – the next place to which the Knight intended to bring terror and chaos. He reached for the hilt of his Energy Sword, slung across his back.

Before he could draw his weapon, a low rumbling filled the air around him. It was a deep, thunderous voice.

'Black Knight!'

The armoured warrior looked up to see the clouds above him boiling. The image of Tenoroc's masked face once again scowled down at him from the sky.

'You have a new mission!' growled Tenoroc. '*Crush* Matt Hatter!'

11

A Score to Settle

Matt watched, mystified, as Roxie once again crouched down to examine a bare patch of ground. She peered at the dusty surface for several seconds, then closed her eyes and inhaled deeply through her nose.

She had been behaving like this ever since their trek had begun – stopping regularly to inspect the rocky terrain. Then she would set out purposefully once more, leaving Gomez and Matt to trudge after her. She hadn't said a word to either of them for a while, though Matt had heard her muttering to herself after peering at the ground or sniffing the air.

'What's she doing?' Matt asked Gomez, quietly

enough that Roxie wouldn't hear. Whatever she was about, it was clear that it required her full concentration. He watched her rise, then stride out again, her eyes scanning the rocky ground ahead.

'Tracking,' replied Gomez, as he and Matt followed. 'Roxie can pick up trails that you and I wouldn't even know were there.'

'OK!' Matt was impressed. *Tracking*, he thought. *That's pretty neat.* He walked beside Gomez in silence for a few more paces. He still hadn't a clue where they were going.

'And . . . *who* are we tracking?'

Gomez looked at him with wide eyes.

'The Black Knight!' he whispered in awe. 'An immortal warrior spirit in a suit of impenetrable Shadow Armour who –'

'– absorbs the skills of other warriors!' finished Matt.

Gomez looked pleasantly surprised. 'You *have* read the *Chronicles*!'

'Nope!' grinned Matt. 'Seen the movie!'

It was called *Knights of the Realm*. He'd watched

it with Zach, ages ago. He remembered glimpsing an old poster for it back in the Coronet's Screen Two corridor, too – back before everything went crazy. The Black Knight had been the best thing in the movie. When it came to bad guys, he was the real deal.

But he's just a movie character, thought Matt. The idea that the Black Knight was *actually* real, that Roxie could somehow track him down – that was a bit crazy, wasn't it?

Their trek had now led them into a gully between two higher areas of the rocky plateau. The steep rock walls to either side were speckled with green lichen. In one, Matt could see the dark arches of several small openings – cave-mouths, or tunnels perhaps. Fallen boulders lay here and there, some small, others taller than Matt.

Roxie had stopped to taste the air again. She called back to Matt and Gomez excitedly.

'We're getting close, guys! These pollutant traces are fairly fresh, I'm sure. We can't be far off now.' She crouched to examine the ground for further

signs. A moment later she triumphantly held up a blackened fingertip. 'See! Another oil droplet!'

Matt turned to Gomez again. 'Where'd she learn all this stuff?'

'It's in her blood,' Gomez explained. 'Roxie comes from a long line of Trackers. Her parents were particularly gifted.' He looked at Matt. 'Her mother was your grandfather's Tracker.'

Grandpa had his own Tracker? thought Matt. He was learning stuff every minute. But something about the way Gomez had spoken of Roxie's parents bothered him. Gomez had used the past tense.

'So, her mom and dad . . .' Matt said quietly. 'They're . . . not around any more, then?'

Gomez shook his head. 'Her mother disappeared during a mission with your grandfather. She was tracking one of Tenoroc's Super Villains across the Sea of Sands – but Tenoroc whipped up a sandstorm to cover his traces. When the storm finally cleared, your grandfather couldn't find any sign of Roxie's mother. When Roxie's dad heard what had happened, he set out alone to track her down.' Gomez's eyes filled with pity. 'Roxie hasn't seen either of them since. That's why she's so determined to bring down Tenoroc. She's got a score to settle.'

Matt couldn't think what to say. *Poor Roxie.*

Suddenly, his thoughts were forced elsewhere. His look of sympathy changed to one of alarm.

'Gomez! Does the Black Knight ride a kind of flying bike?'

'A Hover-Charger, yeah,' confirmed Gomez. He chuckled. 'Let me guess – the movie?'

'No . . .' Matt was staring over Gomez's shoulder. He pointed. 'Right there!'

All doubt about the Black Knight being real had vanished from Matt's mind. The terrifying warrior from *Knights of the Realm* was, at this very moment, heading their way . . .

12
Knight Fight

The Black Knight reined in his Hover-Charger.
The robotic steed reared to a halt only metres
from where Matt and Gomez stood. Its artificial eyes
burned red. It let out a horrible high-pitched screech
– an electronic imitation of a horse's whinny.

Matt saw the mounted warrior reach behind his
saddle and grasp something with his right gauntlet.
It looked like a spiked metal club. With a bellow, the
Knight raised it high. A glowing three-metre beam
of flame-bright energy grew from its spiky end.

The Black Knight levelled his glowing lance at
Matt and Gomez. He urged his charger to rear up
again, and let out a mighty roar.

'Defend yourselves!'

Matt and Gomez, terrified and unarmed, were not about to meet the Knight's challenge. They followed their gut instinct – take cover! They dashed behind the nearest of the large boulders that dotted the gulley floor. But as the Black Knight came charging their way, lance in hand, Matt had the sinking feeling that even solid rock wouldn't protect them from the weapon's lethal beam.

'Gomez! Move it!' Matt yelled. Gomez didn't budge. He was paralysed with fear. And the Black Knight was almost upon them . . .

Matt launched himself at Gomez, knocking him to the ground – and out of harm's way. A split second later, the Knight's lance-beam slashed through the boulder. The huge rock disintegrated, exploding into a shower of fragments and dust.

The Black Knight's ferocious charge carried him some distance along the gulley. But by the time Matt was back on his feet, the Knight had already slowed his Hover-Charger enough to turn it round. He was lowering his lance, preparing to charge again.

The armoured warrior bore down on Matt and Gomez for a second time. Gomez, who was still picking himself up, let out a wail of terror. Once again, he froze with fear.

This time, it was Roxie who came to the rescue. She sprang into the path of the speeding Hover-Charger. In one smooth action, she drew her staff from its sheath and triggered it to extend to its full length.

'Gomez! Just *move it*!' she yelled, as the Knight came hurtling their way.

Matt watched in horror. It seemed certain that Roxie was about to be knocked flat. But the next moment she had leapt high into the air, above the charger's path. Twisting in mid-air, she brought her staff

whipping down to strike the Black Knight hard across his armoured chest.

Roxie's brave intervention did little to harm the Knight – but it did prevent him from getting a clear run at her companions. Unfortunately, it cost Roxie dearly. The clash sent her sprawling. Her staff was knocked from her grasp and clattered away across the gulley floor.

The Black Knight brought his Hover-Charger to a halt. He deactivated his lance, stowed its hilt behind his saddle and dismounted. As he stomped straight towards Matt, he reached over one shoulder to draw a huge sword hilt from behind his armoured back. A blade of fiery light blazed from the hilt.

Matt stood rooted to the spot as his enemy advanced. His mind raced. How could *he* possibly fight this monster?

The Black Knight loomed over him. 'Hah!' he thundered. 'A poor excuse for a warrior!' With a swipe of his gauntleted left hand, he knocked Matt flat on his back.

The mighty blow left Matt stunned. He lay helpless on the ground as the Knight advanced, sword raised to strike . . .

13
Plan B

The Black Knight was only a stride away when Matt heard a wild cry from behind his enemy.

'Hi-*yaaaah*!'

The Knight staggered forward, then fell heavily. As he crashed to the ground, his Energy Sword was knocked from his grasp.

The yell was Roxie's. She had recovered her staff, and was back in action. She had surprised the Knight from behind, planting a fierce double-footed kick in his back.

The enraged Knight lumbered to his feet, and turned to confront Roxie. She stood her ground, violet eyes burning.

'In the case of the Black Knight . . .' Roxie gripped her staff determinedly 'the best defence . . .' she took up a martial arts stance, 'is *offence!*'

She sprang into attack, staff whirling. Matt watched in astonishment as she began to rain blow after blow on her armoured opponent. As the Black Knight countered with his mighty fists, Roxie parried, blocked and dodged with incredible speed and agility.

Matt gasped as Roxie ducked another deadly blow, then landed a lightning jab with her staff. Clearly tracking wasn't the only thing Roxie was good at!

Nevertheless, for all her courage, speed and skill, Roxie was no match for the Black Knight. His armour made him all but invincible. Roxie's strikes were having little effect. And the Knight's superhuman strength meant that he had only to land one blow, and the fight would be over.

'Matt!' yelled Roxie breathlessly as she dodged yet again. 'Use your Cell Blaster! It's the only thing that might stop him!'

Matt, still dazed from his fall, looked blank.

'My cell-*what*?'

The fact that Matt had no idea what Roxie was referring to tipped the terrified Gomez over the edge.

'We're doomed!' wailed the Keeper in despair.

But Matt wasn't about to give up on Roxie – cell-thingy or no cell-thingy. There had to be *something* he could do to help her. He looked around desperately for something – *anything* – that he could use as a weapon . . .

Roxie jumped high and slashed at the Knight's neck with her staff. For once, she was too slow. The Knight grasped the staff firmly in his gauntlet. Roxie, gripping its other end, was left dangling in mid-air. The Black Knight swept the staff downward with vicious force. Roxie was flung violently to the ground. She struck her head, and lay still.

With a roar of triumph, the Knight cast Roxie's staff aside and strode forward to stand over her lifeless body. He raised the visor of his spiked helmet – to reveal an inhuman mask of sickly green light.

'Time to claim your fighting skills as my own!' growled the armoured monster.

The Knight's 'eyes' – two brighter patches in his eerie mask – fixed on Roxie's body. It rose to float a little way above the ground. Streams of luminous energy began to pour from it, drawn out by the Knight's staring eyes. As he stood over his victim, the energy streams flooded into his exposed face.

The Knight was so focused on extracting Roxie's life-force that he failed to hear a wild wailing behind him. It was getting closer by the second.

Matt had figured out the 'something' he could do. The idea had flashed into his mind when he spotted the abandoned Hover-Charger. It had taken him a moment or two to reach it, and another few seconds to figure out how to get the thing moving. But now he was in control, driving the charger at full speed towards the Black Knight. Although 'in control' was perhaps not *exactly* accurate . . .

'Waaaaaaaaaaaaahhhhhhhh!'

As the charger swerved and bucked wildly, Matt fought to keep it on target. At the last possible moment, he leapt from the saddle. The charger slammed into the Black Knight's back, sending him flying. Both charger and armoured warrior crashed into the side of the gulley, then hit the deck.

Matt had pulled off a somersault landing and was already on his feet. He and Gomez sprinted over to Roxie's side.

'Roxie!'

For a few horrible seconds, they could get no response. Then, at last, Roxie's eyelids slowly lifted. She looked up at them and gave a faint smile.

'Better late than never!' she said weakly.

Matt and Gomez helped her sit up.

'I don't think he's going to trouble us any more,' said Matt. He doubted even the Black Knight could recover from a collision like that.

But Gomez, who was staring across the canyon, had bad news.

'Don't count on it!'

The Knight was already stirring.

Matt dragged Roxie to her feet. He looked about wildly for a means of escape. His eyes fell on the nearest of the small openings in the gulley's rock wall.

'Time for Plan B,' he said decisively.

Gomez looked at him. 'We *have* a Plan B?'

'Sure . . .'

Matt glanced back at the Black Knight. He had now made his way over to his stricken Hover-Charger and was retrieving the hilt of his lance.

' . . . *run!*' yelled Matt.

He, Roxie and Gomez sprinted towards the cave entrance. Roxie snatched up her staff as she ran.

The Black Knight was already taking aim with the lance hilt.

'There's no escape!' he roared after them. 'That refuge . . .'

He activated his weapon. It fired a single powerful pulse of energy, which rocketed straight towards the fleeing friends. Just as they reached the cave entrance, the energy missile struck the rock above it.

The explosion was devastating. For several seconds, the gulley echoed with the crash and rumble of falling rock. A thick cloud of dust filled the air. When it cleared, all that remained of the cave mouth was a vast heap of fallen rubble.

' . . . shall be your *tomb*!' roared the Black Knight triumphantly.

14
The Chalice of Harmony

Tenoroc clenched a bony fist and let out a gleeful cackle.

'Another Hatter bites the dust!' he crowed.

To his surprise, he had found watching in the Triple Sphere as his young enemy met his doom almost as satisfying as disposing of him personally. He was beginning to feel a little more like his old self.

Craw, nearby, was bobbing up and down with excitement. The little gargoyle had enjoyed watching the fight as much as his evil master.

'Just in time, too!' gabbled Craw, getting rather carried away. 'It looked like the Hatter boy was about to beat . . .'

His voice trailed off as he noticed Tenoroc's scowl. It dawned on him – rather too late – that his hot-tempered master might not appreciate being reminded of the fact that a 'mere child' had nearly given him the slip.

' . . . you,' finished Craw, in a meek squeak. He gave his master a nervous smile, then gulped.

He had already overstepped the mark. Tenoroc had shaped Craw from the Sky Prison's rocks to serve and obey him, not to point out his failings. He decided that the gargoyle would benefit from a gentle reminder of this. With a wicked grin, he swept a hand through the air.

'*From stone you came, in stone you remain!*'

Poor Craw instantly froze. His odd little body became as rigid

as that of an ordinary stone gargoyle. Only his eyes – wide with alarm – still showed signs of life. A pathetic squeak sounded somewhere behind his stone-locked lips.

Tenoroc chuckled. Ignoring his unfortunate underling's muffled protests, he turned back to the Triple Sphere. Now that no Hatter stood in his way, he was eager to put his evil plans into action. It was time to set the Black Knight the terrible task for which he had been reactivated.

Tenoroc pinched a forefinger and thumb close to the glassy surface of the Triple Sphere's crystal orb, then spread them apart. The orb instantly filled with an image of the Knight's visored face.

'Black Knight,' growled Tenoroc, 'this is your quest.'

With another fingertip gesture, Tenoroc called up a second image. It showed a beautiful, jewelled goblet. Its most striking feature was the beam of intense light that poured in a dazzling column from within it.

'The Chalice of Harmony,' hissed Tenoroc,

eyeing the goblet greedily. He knew that he had only to capture the Chalice to bring about the downfall of the first Multiverse realm – the Region of Ruins.

Tenoroc's voice swelled to a roar. 'Find it!' he commanded the Black Knight. '*Claim it!*'

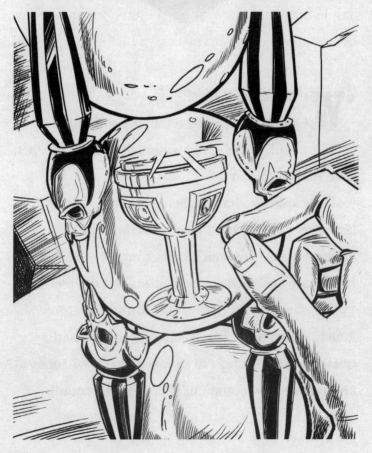

15
The Villain Vault

'We're trapped! *Help!*'

Gomez was having a major panic attack.

'Oh . . . oh . . . oh . . .!' wailed the young Keeper,
trembling with fear.

The explosion had shaken Matt, too. But as the
last echoes of the blast died away, and the dust
began to settle, his shock had given way to relief.
He, Roxie and Gomez were all still in one piece.

The same could not be said of the cave roof.
The blast from the Black Knight's missile had
caused a large section to collapse. A pile of rocks
and rubble now completely blocked the mouth
of the cave.

Matt looked around in the gloom – and realized that this was not, in fact, a cave. It was the beginning of a tunnel. Unfortunately, it had been blocked only a few metres further along by a previous cave-in. Gomez was right. They were trapped.

'I hate confined spaces!' wailed Gomez. 'I – I can't . . . I can't breathe!'

'*Easy*, Gomez.' Matt placed a reassuring hand on his companion's shoulder. Losing their cool wasn't going to help. He tried to think of something to take Gomez's mind off the fix they were in, so that the young Keeper could calm down. 'Tell me about this "Cell Blaster",' he said. 'What is it? And *where* is it?'

'Yeah, Gomez,' said Roxie encouragingly, backing up Matt's efforts to distract him. 'You're the expert on Hatter lore. Fill Matt in, while I find us a way out.' She hurried along the tunnel to the older rockfall, and began using her Tracker skills to examine it.

'O-kaay . . .' Gomez took a deep breath. His

trembling eased a little. He looked at Matt. 'The Cell Blaster is a Hatter's first and last line of defence,' he explained. 'It's a highly adaptable weapon. But more importantly, it can lock villains in the *Chronicles*' Villain Vault.'

Matt frowned. '*Villain Vault*?'

Gomez nodded. 'It's where the Life Cells are stored, in the pages of the *Chronicles*.' He held out a hand for the book. Matt quickly slipped it out of his backpack and passed it to him. As Gomez opened its pages, the amber flash of its cover jewel lit the dingy tunnel.

'Take a look . . .'

Gomez held up a spread from near the centre of the *Chronicles*. Its left-hand page showed a movie poster – for *Knights of the Realm*. On the facing page was a 3D prison cell. Matt peered inside.

'This one's empty.'

Gomez nodded again. 'They *all* are. Tenoroc stole the Life Cells –' he pointed to a blank, hexagonal disc fixed to the cell's bars, ' – and now it's down to *you* to recapture them.'

Matt felt that he was beginning to get his head around this 'Hatter Hero' business. He ran through the basics once more, muttering to himself. 'Let's see . . . Cell Blaster . . . Life Cell . . . Villain Vault.' He grinned at Gomez. 'Gotcha! So – where do we find this Cell Blaster?'

'Right here, in the Region of Ruins!' answered Gomez, eyes shining. He was getting into his stride now. Showing off his Hatter knowledge was what he liked doing best. 'Alfred – your grandpa – knew he was facing almost certain defeat,' he went on. 'So to safeguard the Cell Blaster, he DNA-locked it in solid rock, to await the next Hatter Hero.'

A weapon locked in rock, thought Matt. *Just like the King-sword in* The Curse of Merlin. He looked at Gomez, impressed. 'How come you know all this stuff?'

'Ah, hey . . .' Gomez looked down bashfully. 'It's what we Keepers do.' He closed the *Chronicles*, and handed the book back. Matt had just safely stowed it, when Roxie gave them both an eager call.

'Over here!'

Matt and Gomez hurried to join her. She was crouching near the base of the mound of rubble, holding a small white feather between finger and thumb.

'Watch!' said Roxie.

She let the feather fall. It drifted slowly down the face of the rockfall – then was caught by a current of air, and sucked into a small gap between two rocks.

'There's a through-draught right there! And if *air* is getting through, so can *we*!'

Roxie began scrabbling at the rubble, moving handfuls aside. Within a few moments, she had cleared a large enough gap to push her arm through. She withdrew it, and stood back.

'There's just that one piece blocking the way,' she said, pointing at a single large rock. 'But we'll never shift *that*. It's way too big!'

The rock certainly looked immovable. Matt shrugged. 'You never know till you try!' he said. He reached around the boulder to get a good grip, braced himself, then heaved for all he was worth.

To his astonishment, the rock shifted a little.

'Way to go, Matt!' said Roxie. 'I'd no idea you were so strong!'

Matt stepped back, staring in disbelief at the boulder. He shook his head. 'Me neither!'

Gomez was grinning. '*I* know what's happening!' he said excitedly. 'It's the Multiverse gravity!'

'Huh?' grunted Matt.

'Gravity doesn't work the same here as it does where you come from!' Gomez explained. 'It's complicated – but while you're in the Multiverse, you'll feel stronger. You'll be able to jump higher, run faster –' he pointed at the rock, ' – and shift heavier weights . . .'

'Excellent!' said Roxie. 'A little super-strength is just what's called for right now – cos budging that rock is our only way out of here.' She looked at Matt. 'So get busy, Mr Muscles!'

16

Hatter Trap

'**H**atter's *alive?*'

Tenoroc brought a gnarled fist slamming down on to the rock ledge. The Triple Sphere, in which Matt's image shone, shook with the force of his fury.

'Well . . .' his scowl became a cruel smile.

'. . . I have a remedy for *that!*'

Tenoroc was furious that the Black Knight had failed to get rid of his new Hatter enemy – and more determined than ever to bring about Matt's doom. Setting loose Super Villains from their Life Cells was not the only nasty trick up his sleeve. He could not, at present, use the Triple Sphere

to full effect – but even his reduced powers were
enough to conjure up some deadly mayhem . . .

'*Craw*!' barked Tenoroc. 'Bring me my Space
and Matter Traps!'

Craw didn't move. He couldn't. He was trapped
in his petrified state. His body was still as rigid as
the rock from which it had been crafted. He could
only utter a muffled grunt and roll his eyes.

Tenoroc chuckled mockingly.

'Never mind.'

With a sweep of one hand, he called up the Trap
he required. It rose from the collection of others
scattered across a nearby rock. Each one was a

small, slim, hexagonal disc, very like a Life Cell, but with silver edges instead of gold.

The selected Space and Matter Trap drifted across towards the Triple Sphere. It settled into the socket above the upper orb. As it locked in place, a cloud of liquid light bloomed in each of the Sphere's smaller orbs – red light in the upper one and blue in the lower. The two colours trickled into the main orb, swirling together. As they combined, the entire Triple Sphere began to turn. It spun on its axis like a top, slowly at first, then faster, and faster.

'*Shifting space and matter . . .*' growled Tenoroc, yellow eyes aflame.

17
The Hidden Dimension

It didn't take Matt, Roxie and Gomez very long to clear a big enough gap in the rockfall to squirm through. Once safely past the cave-in, they made steady progress along the tunnel beyond. Roxie took the lead once more.

'We must be in the gem mines,' she told Matt. 'This part of the Region is riddled with mining tunnels. If we follow this one a little way, it should join up with a sled route – one of the bigger tunnels they use to transport gems out of the mine.'

Sure enough, they soon reached a junction with a much wider tunnel, lit by glowing pomegranate-coloured globes hung in pairs from its roof.

A channel had been cut all the way along its rock floor. Resting within this channel was a vehicle that reminded Matt of a mini Roman chariot. It floated just above the ground on a cushion of soft purple light.

Roxie hurried forward, took hold of one side of the hover-sled and began to push.

'Get on!' she instructed. 'This'll take us down to the bottom of the chasm.'

Gomez quickly settled in the back of the sled. Matt gave Roxie a hand getting it moving, then jumped aboard. As the tunnel floor began to slope downwards, the sled quickly picked up speed. Matt gave a whoop of delight as it crested a bump in the track, then set off down an even steeper decline.

'Woo-hoo! Roller-coaster ride! Things are looking up!'

Only moments later, the smile was wiped from his face.

'Look out!' yelled Gomez. 'Flying rocks!'

A hail of airborne boulders was racing to meet them. Before Matt could figure out how a meteor storm could occur in an underground tunnel, the first few rocks came shooting past, forcing him to duck.

'Whoa!'

Matt peered over the front of the sled to see more rocks zooming their way. And these wouldn't miss. He braced himself for the impact.

Instead of the violent crash he expected, there were several loud popping noises. Bizarrely, the rocks were bursting harmlessly against the sled, vanishing like bubbles as they did so.

'Huh?' Matt gave Roxie a bewildered look. 'Is that *normal* here?'

The alarm on Roxie's face told him it wasn't.

'*Error Glitch*!' she cried.

'Tenoroc is manipulating Space and Matter!' squealed Gomez.

'We're caught in a Spatter Trap!' agreed Roxie.

Matt had no idea what either of them was talking about. Whatever it was, though, they clearly considered it bad news.

'Matt!' Roxie grabbed his arm. 'Gomez and

I can't see all the hidden threats! You gotta go Multivision!'

Matt looked at her blankly. 'Go *where*?'

'Just say "going Multivision"!' urged Gomez.

Matt saw little point in arguing.

'*Going Multivision!*'

At Matt's cry, the Multivision Specs came whizzing back across his eyes. As they activated, his entire view was instantly transformed. The mine tunnel ahead dissolved in a whirlpool of colour, to be replaced by a completely different, utterly bizarre landscape.

'What . . . what's happening?'

What Matt was seeing was totally unreal – even by Multiverse standards! The sled was no longer running down a straight sloping tunnel. Instead, it was hurtling down a gigantic helter-skelter of transparent crystal. The glassy track descended in an endless spiral. Its outer edge was supported by slender transparent columns – while the inner one was lined with lethal spikes of sharp crystal.

'We're inside one of Tenoroc's traps, Matt!' cried

Gomez. 'With the Multivision Specs on, you can see the hidden dimension!'

As the sled drifted to the right, it caught one of the spikes. The spike shattered, sending up a shower of deadly shards. Instinctively, Matt tried to force the sled to the left. It responded.

'It's up to you to steer us through it!' yelled Roxie.

A little way ahead, one of the crystal columns suddenly came toppling into their path. Matt flung the sled back to the right to avoid a collision. They made it safely past – just.

'Whoa!' gasped Matt. 'Too close!'

His pulse was racing – and not due to fear alone. Experiencing Tenoroc's Trap in Multivision was breathtakingly exciting. It was like the best ever 3D movie, fairground ride and video game rolled into one – with the nerve-jangling thrill of knowing that the Trap's unreal hazards presented very *real* danger thrown in!

'What do you see, Matt?' asked Roxie.

Something new had just come into view. A group

of five fantastically outlandish winged creatures were coming their way. They were flying in formation, like some sort of attack squadron. Their round orange bodies were covered in crystal spikes.

'Um . . . flying glass . . . *hedgehogs*?' said Matt.

This description was good enough for Gomez. 'No!' wailed the Keeper. '*Crystal Gremlins*!'

The Gremlins dived into the attack, spinning their bodies wildly to fire their crystal body-spikes straight at the speeding hover-sled. Matt threw the sled one way, then the other – and somehow managed to dodge the barrage of glinting missiles.

They had survived a first wave of Crystal Gremlins. Matt seriously doubted they would survive a second.

'What do I do?' he appealed to Roxie and Gomez.

'Look for a fault,' replied Roxie. 'A weakness – our way out!'

But try as he might, Matt couldn't see any such thing. Worse, he spotted something up ahead that made his blood run cold. A solid wall of thick

crystal blocked the spiralling track. If they hit that, going at this speed, they were history.

As the wall raced nearer, Matt's mind raced, too. *Crystal glass . . . crystal glass . . . come on!*

He remembered something from a science lesson about an opera singer who could shatter a crystal wine glass just by –

Of course!

'Crystal Glass!' yelled Matt. He flung his weight to the right, making the hover-sled tilt. Its bottom edge scraped along the glassy floor racing past beneath it. The friction created a loud, piercing screech.

'If you hit just the right pitch . . .' murmured Matt.

As the sled hurtled towards the deadly dead end, Matt adjusted its tilt, trying to keep his nerve. The screech became a clear, high-pitched tone.

' . . . it *shatters*!'

An instant before impact, the wall of crystal ahead exploded. Matt took cover behind the sled's front, forcing Roxie down with him. The sled burst through the chaos of crystal fragments . . .

. . . and was suddenly back in the Region of
Ruins, overground, falling through thin air.

Matt, Roxie and Gomez screamed as the sled
crash-landed. It bounced once, then skidded wildly
across the ground a little way before screeching
to a standstill.

Slowly, Matt and the others picked themselves
up. All three of them were shaken, but unharmed.
The sled, however, had come off rather worse.
Matt stepped out of the wrecked vehicle and gave
it a once over.

'Sled's totalled! *Now* what?'

Roxie wasn't listening. She was already fully
occupied with getting her bearings. The sled had
come to rest on the floor of a sheer-walled canyon.
There were streams and pools of lava nearby. Roxie
sniffed the air, peered at the sky for a moment or
two, then smiled.

'I know where we are!' she declared. 'Follow me!'
And without further explanation, she began to pick
her way purposefully across the canyon floor.

18
The Cell Blaster

Matt wondered where Roxie was leading them. She hadn't as much as paused since setting out along the canyon. She was like a hound on a scent. Matt's feet were beginning to hurt. Thanks to his brush with the Black Knight, the close-shave with the rockfall, and the recent hover-sled wipeout, most of the rest of him ached as well.

Gomez looked weary, too – until Matt saw his face suddenly light up. The Keeper broke into a jog, overtaking Roxie. His eyes were fixed on something up ahead. He stopped short of a large, lone boulder. A narrow beam of sunlight, projected by a crack in the canyon wall, spotlit something

shiny and cylindrical sticking out from the rock's
surface.

'There it is, Matt!' cried Gomez, pointing.
'The Cell Blaster!'

Roxie gave a satisfied smile. She and Matt
hurried to join Gomez.

At first glance, Matt thought the Cell Blaster
looked like something his gadget-mad dad might
have come up with. It was roughly torch-shaped,
with a spherical amber jewel at its narrow end.
Thin tubes ran from the jewel, spiralling around
the Blaster's body. Clear panels on either side
revealed a complex mechanism of cogs and
wheels within.

The Cell Blaster's fatter, hexagonal end was
embedded in the rock. There were circular ripples
around it, as though it had been thrust into place
when the rock was partly molten.

Matt stared at the extraordinary device. It
looked beyond cool. He was desperate to try it out.
He wondered how in the world he was supposed
to remove it. Gomez seemed to read his thoughts.

'All you'll need is courage, strength and focus!'

Hearing this, Roxie pushed past Matt. 'Qualities *I* possess by the bucketload!' she said confidently. She grasped the Cell Blaster with both hands. Gritting her teeth, she began to pull.

'*Hnnnn-uhhh-nnnnnh!*'

Roxie kept up her tugging and grunting for several seconds. The Blaster remained exactly where it was. As she tried one last mighty heave, Roxie's grip slipped and she fell flat on her back.

'Oh . . .' added Gomez, trying to keep a straight face, '. . . and, of course, you need to be a *Hatter*!'

Roxie got to her feet, looking embarrassed. Matt took her place.

'Here goes nothing . . .'

He took a firm two-handed hold on the Cell Blaster, gathered his strength, and pulled for all he was worth.

'*Nnnnnnnnnnnnng!*'

The Cell Blaster didn't budge.

Matt gave it everything he had. But the Blaster didn't feel like it was *ever* going to move, regardless of the extra strength he was supposed to have here in the Multiverse. It was stuck fast, in solid rock. Downhearted, Matt gave up.

But Gomez wasn't about to let him.

'Matt – *focus*!' he urged. '*Believe . . .*'

Matt glared at the Cell Blaster – and found his memory reaching back to his encounter with his grandfather's hologram, in the Screen Two corridor. What had Grandpa told him? *Have faith in yourself.*

'Grandpa . . .' murmured Matt under his breath. 'I *won't* let you down!'

He took hold of the Cell Blaster again, cleared his mind of all thoughts

but one, and pulled.

This time, the Blaster came away from the rock. Yellow light filled the amber jewel at its tip, and flowed along its spiralling tubes. It began to whirr and thrum.

As the freed device activated in his hand, Matt felt a thrilling physical rush. Just like when he had first worn the Multivision Specs, it was as if a missing part of him had been reattached. This must be what being 'DNA-locked' to something felt like!

Matt raised the Blaster triumphantly. Gomez was beaming.

'Hmph!' muttered Roxie. 'I must've loosened it . . .'

With the glowing Cell Blaster in his grasp, Matt felt his confidence swell. For the first time since he had come tumbling into this strange new world, he felt fully equipped and raring to go.

He gave his friends a look of steely determination.

'*Now* we're ready for the Black Knight . . .'

19

Darkness Falls

If Tenoroc had known that the new Hatter Hero had survived his lethal Space and Matter Trap, and had just succeeded in retrieving a weapon to use against him, he would have been in a very black mood.

But for the moment, Tenoroc was unaware of Matt's good fortune. His attention was elsewhere. He was closely following the Black Knight's quest to seize the Chalice of Harmony – and feeling very pleased with himself. The Chalice was almost in his power.

Tenoroc had always seen the peace-loving

Harmonians as easy prey. He had not expected the Black Knight to come up against much resistance from them – and he had been proved right. The Knight had found it easy to force his way into Harmonia's Hall of Light. Only Baccus, the Harmonian Master Scholar, had tried to stop him – by pleading with him to be merciful.

Pitiful old fool! thought Tenoroc. The Black Knight knew nothing of mercy. He had responded to Baccus's pleas by activating his Energy Sword. Baccus and his people had fled in terror.

Now Tenoroc could see in the Triple Sphere's orb that the Knight was approaching the Chalice itself. It stood on a podium at the centre of the Hall of Light. A column of intense white light rose from within it. The beam climbed straight through the centre of the Hall's domed ceiling.

Tenoroc watched eagerly as the Black Knight took up the jewelled lid from beside the Chalice. The Knight reached out to place the lid over the glowing goblet . . .

. . . and then hesitated. He let out a nervous

grunt, and drew back his hands. Despite his fearsome nature, he seemed afraid of the Chalice.

Tenoroc's eyes flashed with fury and impatience.

'Fool!' he snarled. 'Your shadow armour will keep the sacred light from harming you!'

In the Sphere, Tenoroc saw the Black Knight raise his visored face, listening to his master's angry voice.

'Now . . .' growled Tenoroc, '. . . take the Chalice, and let eternal darkness fall!'

Once again, the Black Knight reached out with his gauntleted hands. This time he did not flinch. He covered the Chalice with the lid, extinguishing its glow. The Hall of Light fell into eerie darkness.

The Black Knight seized the Chalice by its stem and raised it triumphantly.

'It is done!' he roared.

And the Hall of Light echoed with Tenoroc's answer – a burst of wild, blood-chilling laughter.

20

Battle on the Bridge

To use the Cell Blaster against the Black Knight, Matt was going to have to find him first. Roxie's instinct was to head straight back to the spot where the Knight had attacked them earlier.

'That way, I can pick up his trail again, no problem,' she said.

Matt looked unconvinced. 'What if his Hover-Charger is still working? He could be miles away by now.'

'Maybe we should go back to Central Hall?' suggested Gomez.

Roxie looked at the Keeper suspiciously. 'You trying to find him, or *avoid* him, Gomez?'

'I wish!' said Gomez miserably. 'But that's not it. What I meant was, well . . . if there have been any more sightings or attacks, news will probably have reached the Council of Elders, won't it? If you're really set on tracking him down, they might be able to tell us where he is . . .'

Roxie and Matt exchanged looks. Gomez had a point.

So with Roxie as guide, they trekked along the bottom of the canyon until they came to the point where the Broken Bridge spanned the gap way up above them.

Matt craned his neck to look up the sheer face of the chasm wall to the promenade and Piazza, far above.

'How the heck do we get up *there*?' he wondered out loud.

In response, Roxie bundled him on to a small stone platform set against the cliff. She and Gomez took their places on either side of him.

'Just don't look down, OK?' Gomez advised Matt in a whisper.

The platform began to climb steadily up the cliff-face. It was propelled by a thin column of lava that rose in a channel in the rock – like mercury rising in a thermometer.

Matt's first experience of the Multiverse had already included quite a few rides: through the portal; on the Black Knight's out-of-control Hover-Charger; in the runaway mine sled. They had all ended the same way – with a major bump. So he was relieved when his lava-lift ride proved less traumatic. By the time the lift reached the level of the promenade, he was a little dizzy from the height but otherwise unscathed.

The three friends stepped off, and headed for the Portico.

'We need to find Baccus,' said Roxie.

'The Master Scholar,' Gomez told Matt. 'He's the most likely to have news about the Black Knight's whereabouts.'

Tracking down their enemy turned out to be rather easier, however, than they had expected.

'There he is!' cried Roxie, pointing ahead.

Matt followed her gaze. A familiar figure in black armour had just emerged from the Portico. He was making his way down the steps to the Piazza, where his Hover-Charger waited. He was clutching something.

'*Look*!' cried Gomez in dismay. 'He's got the Chalice of Harmony!'

'Is that bad?' asked Matt.

'*Bad*?!' Gomez stared at him. 'It's Harmonia's sacred light! Without it, this place will end up like Discordia – a lifeless ruin!'

Matt's eyes filled with grim determination.

'Then we'd better get it back!'

He sprinted for the Piazza, with Roxie and Gomez right behind him. A gravity-scooter was parked close by. The three friends leapt on to it.

Just imagine it's a giant skateboard, Matt told himself. *With no wheels.* With a running kick-start, he sent the scooter gliding swiftly towards their enemy.

The Black Knight had already mounted his Hover-Charger. He turned his visored face their way.

'So – you survived!' he roared at Matt. 'Perhaps

you *are* a worthy warrior.'

The Knight reached for his charger's reins. With a screeching whinny, the mechanical beast darted forward. It zoomed across the Piazza and out along the canyon bridge.

Halfway across the canyon, the bridge met a towering column of rock. Steps wound up it to a small domed temple perched at its top. This was the famous Temple Mount, where Alfred Hatter and Tenoroc had fought their epic battle.

As the Black Knight reached the foot of the Mount, he swung his charger round to face back towards the Piazza. He was still clutching the Chalice in one hand. With the other, he drew his Laser Lance. The lance's glowing beam burst into life. The Knight gave another roar, then came charging back along the bridge.

'Right!' yelled Matt defiantly. 'Bring it on!' He reached for the Cell Blaster on the underside of his backpack. It was time to find out just what his grandfather's old weapon could do. As he grabbed the Blaster, his Multivision Specs activated.

'*Yaaaahhh!*'

With a wild yell, Matt propelled the gravity-scooter forward. It skimmed along the bridge, straight towards the oncoming Hover-Charger.

Gomez was clinging on for dear life. He gave Roxie a terrified look. 'Does . . . does he know what he's doing?' he whispered.

'Nope!' replied Roxie. She drew her staff, ready for combat. 'But he's doing it in *style*!' Unlike Gomez, she was thrilled by Matt's reckless bravery. *Now* he was acting like a Hatter Hero!

Matt, though, was having problems. He was fumbling with the Cell Blaster's handgrip, shaking

and jiggling it. 'How does this thing *work*?' he muttered. Then, as his hand found a comfortable hold, something odd happened. He felt the same strange thrill that had run through him when he drew the Blaster from its rock. A connection formed between him and the device – and its amber jewel flared with light.

'Ah-ha! Got it!'

The Blaster had activated in the nick of time. The Black Knight was almost upon them. As the gravity-scooter and Hover-Charger rushed together, the Knight levelled his glowing lance at Matt's body.

Through the Multivision Specs, Matt seemed to see everything more sharply. With lightning speed, he took aim with the Cell Blaster. A burst of fizzling green energy shot from its hexagonal end. It struck the Knight's right arm. With a roar of anger, he dropped his Laser Lance.

'Rox!' yelled Matt. 'The Chalice!'

Roxie sprang from the speeding scooter in a high, acrobatic leap. From mid-air, she swiped at the Black Knight's left gauntlet with her staff. As the Hover-Charger and scooter shot narrowly past one another, Roxie's blow sent the Chalice flying from the Knight's grip.

Gomez, too, had jumped from the scooter. The Chalice went arcing through the air, straight towards him. He stretched high to grasp it.

Matt brought the scooter to a halt. He jumped off, and hurried to the Keeper's side.

'Nice catch, Gomez!'

Roxie joined them. She stowed her staff, then grabbed the Chalice from Gomez. She was eager to release its life-giving light. But as she took hold of

its cover, Gomez gave a warning shriek.

'*Roxie* – don't open it! The light will blind you!'

By now the Black Knight had swung his robotic steed around. He was heading back along the bridge towards them. He brought the Hover-Charger to a halt, and dismounted. With a roar, he drew his Energy Sword. As its glowing blade activated, he advanced.

Matt stepped bravely forward to confront him.

'You up for round two?' he said breezily. 'Or have you had enough?'

The Black Knight let out a growl of scorn. He raised his weapon.

'Those brave words,' he thundered, 'shall be your *last*!'

Matt looked up at the mighty warrior towering over him, with his glowing sword ready to strike. He had a horrible feeling that the Black Knight might be right.

21

A New Hatter Hero

Matt steeled himself as the Black Knight loomed over him. Now was not the time to lose his cool.

'Quick, Gomez!' he hissed. 'How do I beat this guy?' He was hoping that if anyone knew the Knight's weakness, it would be the fact-mad Keeper. 'What's the chink in his armour?'

Gomez looked miserable. 'There isn't one!' he wailed. 'Only intense light can harm him – but with his shadow armour on, *he's invincible*!'

'Great!' Matt swallowed dryly. '*Now* you tell me!'

With a roar, the Black Knight took a mighty swing with his sword. Matt instinctively raised the

Cell Blaster. Its jewel lit once more, and a twisting blade of green energy, like the spiral of a corkscrew, grew from its tip. Matt used it to block the Knight's deadly blow.

The Knight brought his sword slicing down again . . . and again. Matt managed to deflect the blows with his own unique weapon. But he knew he could not hold out for long against so powerful an opponent. His mind raced, desperately seeking a way to avoid defeat. *What had Gomez just said?* That the Knight was invincible *with his armour on*. An idea sprang into Matt's mind. *Yes, that might* just *work . . .*

As the Black Knight attacked again, Matt staggered back under the weight of his blow. He fell backwards against the bridge's stone parapet. He lay still, eyes closed. The Cell Blaster slipped from his limp grip. The Multivision Specs deactivated.

'Matt!' yelled Roxie.

'*No!*' cried Gomez in despair. He screamed angrily at the Black Knight. 'What have you done!?'

The Knight paid no attention. He simply sheathed his weapon, and strode over to where his victim lay.

Standing over Matt's body, he lifted the visor of his helmet to reveal the mask of light beneath.

'Your fighting skills – *are mine*!' he roared triumphantly.

He stooped over Matt, preparing to drain his life-force.

One of Matt's eyelids lifted a fraction – just enough for him to check that his plan was working. He had realized that the Black Knight would have to open his armour's visor to claim Matt's life-force. And that gave Matt his one and only chance.

In a flash, he was back in action. The Multivision Specs reactivated even as his eyes flew fully open.

'Rox!' he yelled, thrusting out a hand. 'The Chalice!'

Roxie was quick to understand. She tossed the Chalice of Harmony Matt's way. He caught it and yanked off its cover. A stream of intense light poured out. With his own eyes protected by the Multivision Specs, Matt aimed the dazzling beam straight at the Black Knight's open visor.

'Waaaarrrrrrrrgggggghhhh!' The Black Knight's
howl echoed across the canyon. 'It *burns*!'
His armoured body thrashed wildly. It seemed
unable to escape the beam's hold. To Matt's
astonishment, the stream of light lifted the Knight
from the ground, suspending him helplessly in the

air. Matt kept the Chalice's beam aimed at the Knight's unprotected face. The warrior's form began to fade and flicker.

'He's going hologram!' cried Gomez. 'Book him, Matt!'

Matt remembered the flashback the *Chronicles* had shown him – of his grandfather tackling the Mummy. Quickly, he re-capped the Chalice and set it aside. He reached for the Cell Blaster. It thrummed into life as he picked it up.

Matt took aim. A fizzling white beam burst from the Blaster. It shot out towards the Black Knight's floating holographic form. Slowly but surely, it began to reel it in. The Blaster bucked and shook in Matt's hand as its beam dragged the shrinking hologram closer and closer.

'Victory . . . is . . . *yours* . . . Hatter!' roared the helpless Knight.

In a final fizzing rush, the hologram vanished completely, swallowed up by the Cell Blaster. The energy beam cut out.

Matt stared at the Blaster in amazement, not

entirely sure what he had just done. There was something different about the device's tip. Its previously blank face now held a gold-edged hexagonal disc. A Life Cell. It showed a frozen image of the Black Knight.

Once again, Matt acted on an instinct he didn't fully understand. He slipped the *Chronicles* from his backpack, and pressed the Blaster's tip against the matching-shaped jewel on the book's cover. With a twist, he locked the Blaster in place. The cover jewel glowed brightly for a moment. Then the Cell Blaster released itself. The Life Cell had gone. Matt could see it sinking slowly into the *Chronicles*' fading jewel.

Matt stowed the Cell Blaster beneath his pack, then eagerly opened the *Chronicles* – to the same page Gomez had shown him in the mine tunnel. The barred prison cell was no longer empty. It was occupied by a figure in black armour. The imprisoned Knight tugged hopelessly at the bars of his cell and let out a roar of frustration and fury.

As Roxie and Gomez came rushing over, Matt slammed the *Chronicles* shut. The Multivision Specs deactivated. Matt's blue eyes sparkled with delight and relief.

'We did it!'

'*Woo-hoo*!' whooped Roxie, high-fiving him.

'That's one Super Villain, back where he belongs – in the Villain Vault!' grinned Gomez.

Somehow, working together, they had booked their first bad guy.

22

A Vow of Revenge

Tenoroc leant heavily on the rock ledge on which the Triple Sphere stood. He was hunched over, and breathing with difficulty. He stared in disbelief at the image in the Triple Sphere's orb – of Matt, Roxie and Gomez celebrating the Black Knight's defeat.

'*Again* a Hatter wrecks my plans!' Tenoroc wheezed weakly.

He was struggling to come to terms with the fact that an enemy so young had outwitted him. Matt had wrecked his scheme to destroy the Region of Ruins. He had captured one of his strongest allies – one of the Life Cells' occupants on whom

Tenoroc was relying for his return to power.
The evil overlord had been weakened by this loss.
His efforts to create chaos in the Multiverse had
left him exhausted.

Tenoroc, however, was not one to admit defeat
lightly. Though close to collapse, he somehow
found enough strength to bring a gnarled fist
slamming down.

'But I will send *more* villains – bigger, stronger and even more powerful than the Black Knight!' he hissed, eyes full of rage.

Then his body sagged once more.

'As soon as my strength returns . . .' he muttered weakly.

Craw was watching from where he stood, statue-like, nearby. The curse that had left the unlucky gargoyle rock-solid had weakened slightly as Tenoroc's energy failed – but Craw could still barely move. With great effort, he shimmied comically forward a little way.

'M-m-master?' he stammered though stiff lips. 'Y-you still have enough power to free *me* . . .'

The little gargoyle tried to take another lurching step, but only managed to wobble on the spot. He rocked to a stone-stiff standstill and gazed pathetically at Tenoroc's slumped form.

' . . . *haven't you?*'

23
Matt's Task

Matt, Roxie and Gomez were still celebrating their victory, when the *Chronicles'* amber jewel suddenly flared with light. Matt held out the book to look at the glowing gemstone – and saw a familiar holographic figure materialize above its front cover.

'*Grandpa!*'

The last time the *Chronicles* had projected his grandfather's image, Matt had been unable to get any kind of response from the hologram. Communication had been one-way. This time, things were different.

'*Matthew?*' The old man peered at Matt,

adjusting his glasses as if unsure he was seeing properly. He raised one bushy white eyebrow. '*You're* the next Hatter Hero?'

Matt was over the moon to have the chance to talk to his grandfather. He was still buzzing from the fight, too. 'I know! It's crazy! It was a mistake!' he gabbled. 'But I just booked the Black Knight!'

Matt's grandfather beamed. He swung a clenched fist in a *that's-my-boy* way. 'Well *done*, Matt!' he cried. Then his expression became serious. 'Listen – it's now down to *you* to keep the Multiverse safe,' he said gravely. 'But first and foremost you *must* take care of yourself!'

Matt, however, had his own top priority.

'But how do I save *you*, Grandpa?'

Even as Matt asked his burning question, the projection began to fade.

'*Grandpa!*' cried Matt.

The hologram had vanished before his grandfather could reply. The light in the *Chronicles'* jewel blinked out. Matt hung his head.

But the appearance of the hologram, however brief, seemed to have cheered Gomez no end. 'Don't you see, Matt?' he said. 'The weaker Tenoroc gets, the *stronger* your grandpa gets!'

'Until he's strong enough to bust out of that prison!' agreed Roxie.

Matt considered this. Foiling Tenoroc's plan by booking the Black Knight certainly seemed to have boosted his grandfather's ability to communicate with him. *Grandpa could see me, and hear me,* he thought. His spirits lifted.

Then the true scale of the task ahead of him suddenly struck home.

'So – I have to book *all* the villains to free Grandpa?' Matt looked downcast again. 'How can I do that all on my own?'

Roxie's ordinarily feisty look was replaced by one of real warmth. 'You're not on your own, Matt,' she said gently.

'That's right!' said Gomez. 'You have *us*!'

Matt smiled gratefully at his two newfound friends. He held out an open palm. Roxie and Gomez each placed a hand on his. Matt felt less daunted by his mission knowing that they would tackle it as a team.

There was a swishing noise in the air above them. The three friends looked up. From a patch of sky just above Temple Mount, a tube of swirling purple light was snaking down towards them.

Matt nodded. 'Better go make my excuses . . .' As the portal drew nearer, his Multivision Specs activated. He jogged across to jump lightly on to the bridge's opposite parapet, then turned to give his friends a wave. 'See you soon!'

'Remember, Matt . . .' Roxie called after him, 'the Multiverse *has* to remain a secret!'

'Got it!' Matt yelled back. Then, with a final salute, he leapt up into the mouth of the portal. In an instant, he was whisked away along its whirling vortex . . .

. . . and in the next moment, the sky over Temple Mount was calm and clear once more.

24

Almost the Truth

'And where have *you* been for the last two hours?'

Matt's mum confronted him as he burst through the doors into the Coronet's lobby.

Matt stared at her, temporarily lost for words. He had realized, of course, that his absence was unlikely to go unnoticed. His return journey along the Screen Two corridor and through the revolving bookcase had not taken long. He had been as quick as he could stowing the *Chronicles* safely up in his turret room. But he had been away in the Multiverse for quite some time. His parents were bound to want to know what he'd been up to.

What had thrown Matt now was the exact wording of his mum's interrogation. *Two hours.* He was certain he had spent a *lot* longer than that in the Region of Ruins. Then he remembered what Gomez had told him about how gravity worked differently in the Multiverse. *I guess it's the same thing with time,* thought Matt.

For a moment, he considered telling his mum the truth. He wondered how she would react if he told her, honestly, that he had just ridden an inter-dimensional portal back from another world where he had overcome a cinematic Super Villain. He was pretty sure that wouldn't go down well.

Besides, Roxie had made it very clear. She had told Matt it was vital to keep the Multiverse a secret. Matt planned to tell Marlon all about his fantastic adventure, of course. But he was confident that his little furry pal would keep it to himself. As far as everyone else was concerned, the less they knew, the better.

His mum was still waiting for an answer.

'Erm . . .' began Matt. He knew it would be best

to stick to at least a *version* of the truth. His mum had an uncanny knack of knowing when he was lying. 'I've . . . er . . . been looking for Grandpa . . .' he stammered. 'And I . . . I found a message from him.'

'Oh, yes?' Matt's dad popped up from behind the ticket counter. He was holding a screwdriver. And a roll of tape. And a whisk. It looked like he was trying get the popcorn machine working.

'Uh-huh,' said Matt. 'Something about . . . being stuck on the other side of the world . . . '

Matt was spared from having to expand any further on his story – by his trusty pal, Marlon. The little Tasmanian devil burst into view inside the popcorn machine. He'd been tunnelling in its mountain of popcorn. Through a mouthful, Marlon gave a spluttering chitter to welcome back his best friend.

Matt chuckled. 'I see Marlon's made himself right at home.'

His mum smiled. 'The theatre *is* our home now, Matt.'

Matt's dad came out from behind the counter. 'And all we have to do,' he added cheerily, 'is keep it safe until Grandpa gets back!'

Matt thought of his grandfather, trapped who-knew-where in the Multiverse. He thought of Tenoroc's host of fearsome Super Villains – the villains that he, Roxie and Gomez would have to defeat before his grandfather could escape his prison dimension. He smiled to himself.

'Is that all?' he said, under his breath.